Dear Parent:
Your child's love of reading starts here!

Every child learns to read in a different way and at his or her own speed. Some go back and forth between reading levels and read favorite books again and again. Others read through each level in order. You can help your young reader improve and become more confident by encouraging his or her own interests and abilities. From books your child reads with you to the first books he or she reads alone, there are I Can Read Books for every stage of reading:

SHARED READING
Basic language, word repetition, and whimsical illustrations, ideal for sharing with your emergent reader

BEGINNING READING
Short sentences, familiar words, and simple concepts for children eager to read on their own

READING WITH HELP
Engaging stories, longer sentences, and language play for developing readers

READING ALONE
Complex plots, challenging vocabulary, and high-interest topics for the independent reader

ADVANCED READING
Short paragraphs, chapters, and exciting themes for the perfect bridge to chapter books

I Can Read Books have introduced children to the joy of reading since 1957. Featuring award-winning authors and illustrators and a fabulous cast of beloved characters, I Can Read Books set the standard for beginning readers.

A lifetime of discovery begins with the magical words "I Can Read!"

Visit www.icanread.com for information
on enriching your child's reading experience.

For Anna Franceschelli

HarperCollins®, 🐾®, and I Can Read Book® are trademarks of HarperCollins Publishers.

Dirk Bones and the Mystery of the Haunted House Copyright © 2006 by Doug Cushman All rights reserved. No part of this book may be used or reproduced in any manner whatsoever without written permission except in the case of brief quotations embodied in critical articles and reviews. Manufactured in China. For information address HarperCollins Children's Books, a division of HarperCollins Publishers, 195 Broadway, New York, NY 10007.

www.icanread.com

Library of Congress Cataloging-in-Publication Data
Cushman, Doug.
    Dirk Bones and the mystery of the haunted house / story and pictures by Doug Cushman.— 1st ed.
        p.   cm. — (An I can read book)
    Summary: "Ghostly Tombs" newspaper reporter Dirk Bones, who also happens to be a skeleton, investigates when a pair of ghosts fears that they are being haunted.
    ISBN 978-0-06-073764-1 (trade bdg.) — ISBN 978-0-06-073765-8 (lib. bdg.) — ISBN 978-0-06-073767-2 (pbk.)
    [1. Haunted houses—Fiction. 2. Mystery and detective stories.] I. Title. II. Series.
PZ7.C959Dir 2006
[E]—dc22
                                                                                                2005019484

14 15 SCP 10 9 8 7
❖ First Edition

DIRK BONES
and the Mystery of the
Haunted House

story and pictures by
Doug Cushman

HarperCollins*Publishers*

Clickity click!

Clackity-click! Ding!

This is my typewriter.

My name is Dirk Bones.

I live in the town of Ghostly.

I am a reporter

for the town newspaper,

The Ghostly Tombs.

I look for all the facts

for my stories.

Sometimes I solve mysteries.

One night

my boss came into my office.

"I have a story for you," he said.

"A house on Ghoul Street is haunted."

"That's not news," I said.

"EVERY house in Ghostly

is haunted."

"The ghosts that live
in the Ghoul Street house
say another ghost is haunting them!"
said my boss.
"Now, *that's* news!" I said.
I grabbed my notebook.
"I'm on my way!"

The night was cold.

The wind howled through the trees.

I held on to my hat.

The house on Ghoul Street

was dark and spooky.

I rang the doorbell.

Two ghosts opened the door.

"I am Dirk Bones
from the newspaper," I said.

"I want to write a story
about your haunted house."

"It's so scary!" said one ghost.

"There must be another ghost
making spooky sounds,
but we can't see it."

"They are not ghostly sounds,"
said the other ghost.

"That is why we are so scared."

"What are the sounds?" I asked.

"*Clack, cluckity-cluck bing,
blub, blub,*" said the first ghost.

"No," said the second ghost.

"It's *click, cluck-clackity cling,
flub, flub.*"

"Where do the sounds come from?"
I asked.

"In the cellar," said both ghosts.

"But we can't find anything there."

"I will check for clues," I said.

I went down to the cellar.

The stairs creaked.

I heard *drip, drip, drip*

from a leaky pipe,

but that was all.

"Very strange," I said.

Suddenly I heard another sound.

Click, click, clickity!

I looked around.

No one was there.

Click, clickity-click ding,

glub, glub!

It came from behind the wall.

There was no way to get

to the other side.

"I will check outside

the house," I said.

I went upstairs and then outside.

The wind howled through the trees.

It blew my hat off my head.

I chased my hat to a graveyard

next door to the house.

It was the spookiest graveyard

in the whole town.

I walked around slowly,

looking for my hat.

I spied it behind a flower pot.

I reached down to get it.

Suddenly I heard

clackity, clackity, clack!

A furry paw grabbed my hand!

"Yikes!" I cried.

"Hush!" said a voice.

"It will hear you."

"Wallace!" I said.

"What are you doing here?"

"I was taking a walk

through the graveyard,"

said Wallace.

"Suddenly I heard a spooky noise.

It was not a ghostly noise.

I was too scared to move!"

"I heard the noise too," I said.

"It went *clackity, clackity, clack*."

"That was my teeth," said Wallace.

"The sound I heard was
*click, clickity-click ding,
glug, glug!*

It came from over there."

He pointed to an old tomb.

"I'm going inside," I said.

"I need all the facts for my story."

"Be careful," said Wallace.

23

I went inside the tomb.

I went down some stairs.

"This tomb is bigger

than I thought," I said.

I walked down a long tunnel.

It was very dark.

Suddenly I heard
click, clickity-click, ding,
glug, glug!
I saw a light ahead.
It came from under a large door.
Slowly, I opened the door.

Click, clickity-click, ding,

glug, glug!

"Oh my!" I cried.

A vampire was sitting at a desk.

He was writing on a typewriter.

Next to him was a pot

of bubbling soup.

He jumped.

"Oh!" he said.

"You scared me!"

"Who are you?" I asked.

"My name is Sherman,"
said the vampire.

"I am writing a cookbook.
This recipe is for bat foot stew
with crispy worm brains.
Have a taste."

"Yummy!" I said.

"But what are you doing
in this tomb?"

"I need a quiet place to write,"
said Sherman.

"This tomb is perfect."

"The ghosts next door

can hear you," I said.

"They are scared of your sounds!"

"I meant no harm," said Sherman.

"I'll explain it to them," I said.

"They will not be scared anymore."

I took out my notebook.

"This will make a good story

for the newspaper,"

I said.

"Tell me about your cookbook."

We talked all night.

The next evening my boss
came into my office.
"You wrote a great story
about Sherman," he said.
"Now I have another story.
There is a werewolf in town
who is afraid of the moon!"
"Here we go again," I said.